PINK ME UP

by Charise Mericle Harper

Alfred A. Knopf
New York

For Ava, I can't wait to see you pink up your daddy (my brother) —C.M.H.

THIS IS A BORZOI BOOK PUBLISHED BY ALFRED A. KNOPF

Copyright © 2010 by Charise Mericle Harper

All rights reserved. Published in the United States by Alfred A. Knopf, an imprint of Random House Children's Books, a division of Random House, Inc., New York.

Knopf, Borzoi Books, and the colophon are registered trademarks of Random House, Inc.

Visit us on the Web! www.randomhouse.com/kids

Educators and librarians, for a variety of teaching tools, visit us at www.randomhouse.com/teachers

Library of Congress Cataloging-in-Publication Data
Harper, Charise Mericle.
Pink me up / by Charise Mericle Harper. — 1st ed.
p. cm.
Summary: When Mama is too sick to go to the Pink Girls Pink-nic with Violet, Daddy offers to take her place but, first, he needs to "pink up" his clothes.
ISBN 978-0-375-85607-5 (trade) — ISBN 978-0-375-95607-2 (lib. bdg.)
[1. Pink—Fiction. 2. Fathers and daughters—Fiction. 3. Picnics—Fiction.] I. Title.
PZ7.H231323Pin 2010
[E]—dc22
2009023168

The illustrations in this book were created using acrylic on illustration paper.

MANUFACTURED IN MALAYSIA
April 2010
10 9 8 7 6 5 4 3 2 1

First Edition

Today is a special Mama-and-me day.
Today is the day of the PINK GIRLS PINK-NIC.

Please Join Us
For The
3RD ANNUAL
Pink Girls Pink-nic
2PM   Maple Grove Park
Please Wear Pink

We will be . . .

First, I set up Mama's clothes.

Together, we will be *beautiful*.

Then . . .

OUR LITTLE BUNNIES ♥

Violet Stan Simon Adam Everet Wilson Monty Virgil Rex

Wake up, Mama!
I'm ready to go.

Why is Mama wearing pink spots?

Did you put them on special for the party?

Oh no! Mama is sick.
She cannot go to our pink-nic.

Today is the worst day

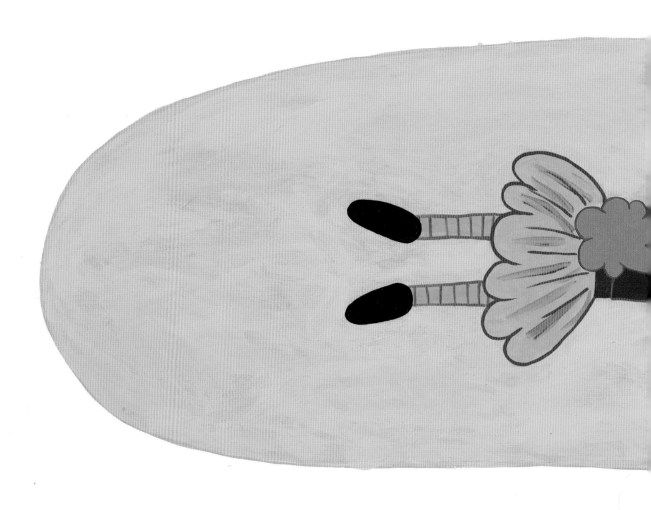

"What if someone else takes you?" asks Mama.

who—Pinky?

Pinky is the only other girl in our house. Pinky will not get dressed up. I have tried that before.

COME ON, Pinky, it's a cute hat.

ROWRRR

"No, someone much more fun," says Mama.

"No, Silly," says Daddy. "It's me.
I will take you."

I tell Daddy something very important:

Daddy! you're a boy!

And it's a
PINK girl
party!

Boys are
NOT
pink!

"Are you sure?" asks Daddy. "I think boys can be pink. Wait, I have something to show you!"

Daddy searches inside his closet. He finds . . .

one pink tie.

But Daddy is hardly pink at all.

"Don't worry," says Daddy. "We just have to pink me up. I bet I can be as pink as you."

Can I make my daddy pink? Let's see . . .

We draw polka dots on Daddy's shirt.

We tape stripes to Daddy's pants.

Daddy should not wear Mama's skirt.

We wrap paper on Daddy's shoes.

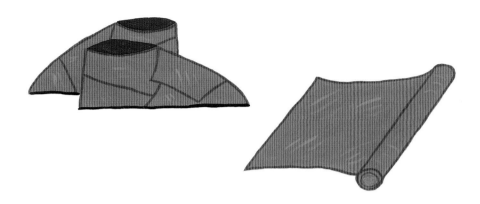

We put stickers on Daddy's jacket.

Now Daddy is . . .

perfectly PINK.

But not as pink as me!

I hold Daddy's hand because he is not used to being pink.
"Don't worry, Daddy. Being pink will be fun," I tell him.

We have the best day—
EVER!

Now all the girls want to **PINK UP**
their daddies, just like me.

I can hardly wait to help Daddy
get ready for work tomorrow.

Then I'll pink up—EVERYTHING!

And we'll all live *pinkishly* ever after.